W

"I couldn't believe it when I arrived at school for the first time. Everyone looking all proper and stuff. It was like an Old Navy commercial. Were there any skaters at this school?"

GAVIN COLE
Age: 13
Hometown: Philadelphia

STONE ARCH BOOKS
presents

written by
BLAKE A. HOENA

images by
FERNANDO CANO AND **OMAR LOZANO**

a
CAPSTONE
production

Published by Stone Arch Books
A Capstone Imprint
1710 Roe Crest Drive, North Mankato, Minnesota 56003
www.capstonepub.com

Printed in the United States of America in Stevens Point,
Wisconsin.   032013   007227WZF13

Library of Congress Cataloging-in-Publication Data is
available on the Library of Congress website.
Hardcover: 978-1-4342-4086-6
Paperback: 978-1-4342-6188-5

Summary: Gavin Cole uses his fix-it skills to find a place with
the skaters at his new school.

Designer: Bob Lentz
Creative Director: Heather Kindseth

Design Elements: Shutterstock

CHAPTERS

Gavin Cole was the last one left on the school bus. He had taken his time grabbing his things to let the other kids get off first. Now it was just him and the bus driver.

"This is the end of the line," she said, with a hint of impatience. She looked back through the big rearview mirror. "Time to get off."

"Yeah, yeah," Gavin replied. "I just dropped something."

That last part was actually a lie. But also, this really wasn't his school — at least not the school his friends went to. It wasn't the one he went to last year. It wasn't even the one he went to just last week.

Gavin felt a little timid about getting off the bus. He didn't know what to expect at this new school. He didn't know if he'd fit in or find a crew to hang with. All he knew, and all his mom cared about, was that he was now far away from the troublemakers back at his old school. Most of those "troublemakers" happened to be his friends.

Sighing out a big breath, he put in his earbuds and cranked the volume. Public Enemy — old school. It seemed fitting since that's where he wanted to be: his old school in the city. Gavin lowered his head and strode to the front of the bus. He didn't look up again until his shoes hit pavement.

The school grounds were enormous, spreading out on either side of him. And it was so clean — unlike his old school, which was covered in soot and pigeon poop. There were no broken windows. And there were no weeds sprouting up from cracks on the outdoor basketball court, because there weren't any cracks. Next to the hoops, there was even a tennis court, with a net instead of a piece of rope stung between the posts. Everything looked so new.

Then there were the other students. They all looked shiny and new, too. Gavin didn't see any torn jeans or faded Ts. No

one had 'fros or even ball caps. Their khakis were ironed, and their shoelaces tied. Gavin kind of felt like he had entered an Old Navy commercial. Looking down at himself, Gavin felt like a mess. His Birdhouse T-shirt was faded. His jeans were frayed around the cuffs. His shoes were scuffed from where they had bit pavement.

Gavin felt pairs of eyes begin to turn in his direction. It didn't help that he was gawking like a tourist. So he slowly drifted toward the school entrance as he tried to ignore the kids watching him. When the bell rang, he acted like he belonged there and casually joined the flow of students.

Once inside, Gavin pulled a note from his pocket. The crumpled piece of paper read, "Homeroom #130." Finding the room took awhile. He didn't want to look dumb and ask anyone where it was, so he just wandered around until he was one of the last few in the hallway.

The room he walked into was much different than the scene on the schoolyard. The kids here were like him, a little rougher around the edges than the kids he saw outside. And they were a kaleidoscope of whites, African Americans, Asians, and Latinos.

The teacher walked in and introduced himself as Mr. Muñoz. "We have a new student today," he said. "Everyone welcome Gavin Cole."

Gavin flushed as the other students, as one, said hello in their various accents.

"Since you're new to this school, Gavin," Mr. Muñoz said. "We'll have someone show you around today. Volunteers? Anyone have first period free?"

Looking behind him, Gavin saw an Asian girl raise her hand. "Okay, Lindsey, can you show Gavin to his locker and give him the tour?" Mr. Muñoz said.

"Sure," was her brief reply.

Mr. Muñoz quickly took roll and read off some announcements about upcoming school events, and then everyone was off to their first-period classes.

Lindsey waited for Gavin outside the door. He was surprised at her size. He felt like a giant compared to her. He was about to comment on that, but the goofy smirk on his face must have tipped Lindsey off.

"No cute little China girl crap, okay," She snapped. "I'm Hmong. Got it?"

"Got it," Gavin said.

"And if you mess with me, my fifteen brothers will kick your butt," she said.

"Wait, what? Fifteen, really?" Gavin said.

Lindsey spun away from him and began walking down the hallway.

"Just kidding. I'm an only child," she said with a smirk. "But you're kinda scrawny. I could take you myself."

Gavin chased after her, toward a row of lockers. She went to one, spun the dial a couple of times, and it opened.

"This is yours," she said.

"But you know the combination?" Gavin asked.

"It was Mike's," she said. "He was a friend."

"Mike?" Gavin asked.

"Yeah, the kid you're replacing in the exchange program," Lindsey said.

For his last year in middle school, Gavin's mom had registered him in a program where inner-city kids could swap schools with students from the 'burbs. The program was more of a one-way street. The suburb kids didn't want to ride on a bus for an hour or longer, just to get to school. So in the end, there was very little "exchanging" going on, which meant there were very few slots open for kids like him.

Gavin's name hadn't been picked with the first round of selections. No one from his school had been chosen. His mom complained, and the next thing he knew, he was on top of the program's waiting list. A few weeks after the school year began, he was here.

"So what happened to Mike?" Gavin asked.

"He got kicked out for fighting," Lindsey replied.

"That was dumb of him," Gavin said.

"Yeah, let's see how easy it is for you here," she said. "If you haven't figured it out yet, we stand out a little here."

"Why, just because we're not white?" Gavin asked.

"The only color that matters here is green," Lindsey said.

Her comment made Gavin even more aware of his frayed cuffs and faded T-shirt.

* * *

The rest of the day went almost like any ordinary school day for Gavin, until lunch. He had eaten with a group of kids that he remembered seeing in homeroom. When he finished, he stepped outside to get a breath of fresh air. A group of guys were starting a pick-up game of basketball.

"It's three on four," one of the three said.

"Tim can sit out," one of the four said.

"Hey, why do I always have to sit out?" Tim asked.

Then one of guys spotted Gavin. "We'll take the new kid."

Gavin knew what was coming. The three had big grins and were looking at him like they had already won the game. The four had an "Oh crap" look on their faces.

When it came down to it, though, Gavin hardly had any skills on the court. Sure, he could hold his own, was athletic, and had a couple inches on some of the guys he was playing against. But he missed an easy layup, bobbled a couple passes, and threw up an air ball from just outside the paint. His side won, but he wasn't the reason.

"Hey, man," one of the three approached him afterward. "I thought you could play."

"Why, because I'm tall?" Gavin shot back. "Or because I'm black?"

The words were out of his mouth before Gavin could stop them. He was just so used to people assuming he could play basketball because he was tall for his age and because of his skin color. It annoyed him to the point that he got smart-alecky about it, without thinking, anytime someone made a comment about his lack of skills on the court.

At first, the kid look stunned, but then slowly, his eyes narrowed and his jaw tensed. He was getting angry. That's when Tim stepped in.

"B-ball's not my game either," he said.

Gavin had noticed that Tim was wearing a Quicksilver T-shirt and wondered if he by chance skated, too.

"You skate better than you play?" Tim asked, pointing at Gavin's Birdhouse shirt.

"Yeah, not like that's saying much," Gavin replied.

"Bring your board tomorrow," Tim said. "On Tuesdays, a couple of us head over to the Complex to hit the halfpipe."

"The Complex?" Gavin asked.

"Yeah, the sports complex for our school district. It has an indoor hockey rink and a couple soccer fields. We play all our football and baseball games there. But the coolest thing, there's a pretty awesome skatepark."

"I'll be sure to bring my board," Gavin said with a smile.

For the first time that day, Gavin felt like he might find his place here. There were some skaters, like him. And this Complex sounded intriguing. In all his years of skating, he had never had a chance to drop into a halfpipe before. He was looking forward to it.

The rest of the day went smoothly for Gavin. He sat through the same typical classes he had at his old school. He heard the same typical lectures. He took notes the best he could and realized that he had some catching up to do.

The kids here took their classes more seriously than his friends did. Here, they all had plans to become doctors and lawyers and such. The crew at his old school just hoped to survive another day without crossing the wrong person.

That was one reason his mom had signed him up for the exchange program — to keep him out of trouble. She also wanted him to go to college. What she worried about most was that he'd take after his friends, who cared more about hoops than school.

When she started her standard speech that good grades — not basketball — were the way to get into college, all Gavin could do was listen. She didn't get it that he wasn't like his friends. His grades were good, and he really didn't care that much about b-ball. Skating was his thing.

At the end of the day, Gavin was at his locker when Lindsey came up to him. "So you made it through the first day?" she asked.

"Yeah, but there was a tense moment when some of the guys learned I'm not like Anthony Davis," Gavin replied. "But Tim got me through it."

"Tim?" Lindsey asked, her eyes brightening.

"Yeah, the skater," Gavin said, and that's when he saw the chink in Lindsey's armor. This tough Hmong girl had a thing for skater boys.

"Listen, you live on the north side, right?" she asked.

Gavin nodded. The north side of the city was the low-rent district. The hood. Whatever you called it, the neighborhood was run down and a bit on the rough side.

"Instead of taking the school bus in, meet me at the central bus station," added Lindsey. "The city has an express that stops here in the morning. We can also take it from the Complex to get back to the station."

"Cool," Gavin said.

The bus dropped Gavin off at the corner near his grandmother's apartment. From there, he nearly ran home. He was excited to prep his board for tomorrow.

Once inside, he dashed upstairs, but halfway up he heard his mom call to him from the kitchen.

"How was your first day?" she asked.

"Fine," he replied.

"Just fine?" she asked. "You didn't have any problems finding your classes?"

"No, Mom," he said, his voice spiking with irritation. "Everything was fine."

"Don't take that tone of voice with me, young man," she said. "Dinner will be ready in an hour. We'll talk more about it then."

He was dashing the rest of the way upstairs when he heard her yell something about homework. His board would have to wait until after dinner.

* * *

After he ate, and after his mom grilled him about school, he was ready to work on his favorite board. The decals on it had mostly been worn away. Tape covered the nose, where the deck had splintered after a failed nosegrind. The wheels were mismatched. But it had personality, and he was proud of it. He had pieced it together from parts he picked up at the nearby pawnshop, where he worked a few hours a week.

Actually, his friends thought he was running a skateboard repair shop out of his closet. There were more wheels and trucks and packages of bearings than there were clothes.

As he was examining his board, he heard a familiar *TWAP! TWAP! TWAP!* of basketballs on pavement. Between that, there was the sound of composite wheels carving through the street below his window.

"Gav!" a shout came from outside.

"G-man!" came another.

Gavin rushed to his window. Out on the street, two stories below, was a group of a half dozen kids. His crew. A couple of them had basketballs, and they were all on skateboards — skateboards that he had repaired and pieced together.

They also were all decked out in Tar Heels gear. Last year, one of the high schoolers left to play for UNC, so they all had Rameses ball caps askew on their heads and light blue jerseys on.

"Come shoot some hoops," one of his friends said.

"Can't tonight," Gavin replied.

Another one of his friends turned to the group, "See what I told ya. New school, and he's too cool for us."

A few of the boys nodded in agreement.

Gavin quickly grabbed his skateboard and held it out the window.

"I'm working on one of my boards, guys," he yelled down. "Skating tomorrow."

That silenced the grumblings. His friends all knew how big he was into skating. *And they all should know,* Gavin thought, *working on boards is the only thing that would keep me from shooting hoops with them.*

"Say, Gav, one of my front wheels isn't spinning right," one of his friends yelled up to him. "Could you look it?"

"Yeah, no prob," he replied. "Bring it by tomorrow. It's probably just a bad bearing."

With that, they skated off. His friends weren't pretty on their boards. They wobbled and stumbled over cracks, and more often than not, they had to pick their boards up at the curb. But a couple of them were comfortable enough on their decks to be able to dribble a basketball as they cruised toward the neighborhood courts.

* * *

The next day, Gavin met Lindsey at the central bus station. He was a bit surprised to see a deck poking out from the top of her backpack.

"Dude, pick your jaw up off the ground," she told Gavin. "I skate, too."

"Sorry, I just didn't think . . . I mean, I didn't expect . . ." Gavin felt like he was stumbling over his words.

"Why do you think I didn't roll my eyes and groan

painfully when Mr. Muñoz asked me to show you around yesterday?" she asked, ignoring the fact that she had volunteered. "I could tell you were a skater boy."

Gavin's worries about fitting in at the new school were shrinking further away. He had already found the skater crowd. Now he just needed to prove to them that he could skate and seal the deal.

On the bus to school, Gavin and Lindsey chatted about different tricks. He let her do most of the talking, though. She had practiced at the Complex before, and he wanted to know what the equipment was like.

He had done most of his skating on the street. There weren't any skate parks in his neighborhood. He'd grind along park benches and hop curbs, but rarely did he have a chance to hit any real equipment.

Tim met them when they got off the bus, and he joined in their conversation about different kickflips and grabs. Gavin noticed how Lindsey placed herself strategically between the two boys, so that as he and Tim talked, she was always in Tim's line of sight. The girl had it bad.

"Where's you deck?" Gavin asked.

"I've already dumped it at the office," Tim replied. "See ya later." He headed off by himself.

"What did he mean, 'dumped it at the office'?" Gavin asked Lindsey.

"We have to leave our boards at the office," she explained.

"Why?"

"School policy," she said. "Let's just say kids on skateboards aren't considered ideal students around here. Not to mention, we already have a strike against us for being from the wrong hood, as you would say."

Gavin laughed. If her moves were as quick as her wit, Lindsey must be an awesome skater.

The rest of the day was a confusing blur. Gavin made it to homeroom okay, but unlike yesterday, he didn't have Lindsey as his tour guide, so he got lost a couple times. He stumbled in late to most of his classes, which earned him scowls from the teachers. And then most of the subject matter was beyond what he had learned at his old school. The teachers had been easy on him the first day, but now the gloves were off. So he felt dazed and confused throughout the day. The only thing that kept him motivated was the thought of checking out the skatepark after school.

He found Tim sitting outside during lunch. Today, they sat out the pick-up basketball game. Instead, Tim pointed out the different skaters that would be hitting the park afterward.

There was Derrek, a tall, lanky kid, who stopped by

to say hey. He sounded old school with all the "rads" and "dudes" interspersed in everything he said. Then there was Kirk, who looked like he should be a surfer out on the West Coast. He was blond and buff, and had an arrogant way of strutting around. He had a twin named Kyle, Tim said, but Kyle was nowhere to be seen.

Tim mentioned a handful of other skaters. But he said Derrek and Kirk were the ones to watch when they got to the skate park. The rest were a bunch of posers who only skated because they weren't good at any other sports.

At the end of the day, Gavin met Lindsey by the school office, so they could get their boards back. Outside the main doors, Tim was waiting for them.

"We better get going," he said. "Or the halfpipe line will be a mile long."

As soon as they were off school grounds, three sets of composite wheels hit the pavement. They hopped on their boards and pushed forward. Tim led, with Lindsey close behind. Gavin took up the rear, so he could see if they were serious skaters or not.

In his neighborhood, his friends simply used skateboards

to get around. If you had a bike and locked it up outside, it got ripped off. A skateboard you could carry with you. But his friends were just casual skaters, using their boards to get from point A to point B. They weren't interested in doing tricks.

That wasn't true of Tim and Lindsey. They were skating on a wide bike path. If there was a crack up ahead, Tim would ollie over it. Then Lindsey would. And then Gavin. Afterward, Tim would slow down to let Lindsey and Gavin skate ahead, kind of like a game of leapfrog.

At the next crack, Lindsey did a 180 ollie over it. Gavin followed the trick, and so did Tim.

Then she slowed to let Gavin take the lead. He was a little nervous because now he was being watched. But that didn't mean he couldn't step it up a notch.

Up ahead, he saw a crack in trail. He popped his board up and used his back foot to spin the board around in a 180 underneath him. Then he caught the deck with his feet, landing the pop shuvit on the other side of the crack.

Lindsey mimicked him, but when Tim popped up his board, he kicked too hard, and it spun away from him.

Gavin slowed to let Lindsey by.

"So you aren't a poser after all," she said. "Nice move."

When Tim caught up to him, he motioned Gavin forward. "If ya can't hit the trick, it's to the back of the pack."

Gavin pushed his board forward to chase after Lindsey.

They played this game, trying to match each other's tricks, all the way to the Complex. Gavin was proud that he never once missed a trick. But street skating was his thing. Now the halfpipe, that was another story.

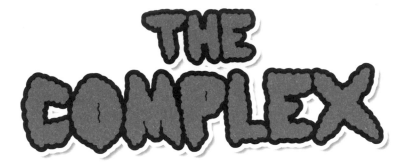

As they approached the Complex, Gavin was awed by it's size. It looked like it might be bigger than their school. It was definitely taller.

Outside the Complex, there was a baseball diamond and fields for soccer and football. Connected to the Complex, he saw the skatepark. He skated up to the fence that surrounded it and looked in. There were the typical spines and rails, launch boxes and banks. But it didn't stop there. A drop-in sat at one end with a mini halfpipe at the other.

Gavin's neighborhood had a small skatepark, but it was nothing like this. The little equipment it had was worn and rusted — hardly safe to use. Not to mention, it just wasn't a safe place to be if you weren't friends with the right people.

An open garage door ran against one wall. Gavin couldn't see what was going on inside, but he could hear the distinct sound of composite wheels carving against wood. Must be skaters on the halfpipe.

"Wipe the drool off your chin, skater boy," Lindsey said.

"Yeah, the best is yet to come," Tim added.

Tim led them through a set of glass double doors. Once they were inside, Gavin saw various signs. One pointed to the tennis courts, another to the indoor soccer field, and still another to an ice rink. Finally, Gavin spotted the sign that pointed to the indoor section of the skate park.

Gavin followed Tim and Lindsey to a counter at the entrance to the skate park. Tim headed to the locker room, where he said he stashed his helmet and pads.

"We have to gear up first," Lindsey said.

She walked over to the counter, where two older guys stood looking bored. They had long hair pulled back in ponytails. They could have been twins if one didn't have blond hair and the other dark hair.

"I'll need a set of pads and a helmet," Lindsey told them.

"That'll be five bucks," the blond-haired guy said as the dark-haired guy turned to pull some elbow and knee pads from the racks behind the counter.

Gavin leaned over to whisper in Lindsey's ear, "Do we need to wear pads?"

She just pointed to a sign on the counter, stating the rules of the park. Rule number one said that all skaters must wear pads and a helmet.

"What do you need?" the blond-haired guy asked Gavin.

"I, um . . ." Gavin stumbled.

"He needs a set of pads and a helmet, too," Lindsey said.

"I don't have any cash on me," Gavin whispered to her.

Lindsey pulled a crinkled punch card from her pocket and handed it to the guy behind the counter. "I'll get his, too."

As the dark-haired guy set the pads and helmets down on the counter, he scanned Gavin up and down. Then he pointed at Gavin's skateboard.

"Can I see that?" he asked.

"Huh, why?" Gavin asked.

His first instinct was to run, like he had done something

wrong. Why would this guy want to be checking out his board? It was his. He didn't steal it.

"I just want to see the work you did on it," he said.

Slowly, embarrassed at the tape and faded decals, Gavin pulled his board from his bag and handed it over to the guy.

"I know it's in rough shape," Gavin said. "But I hope I can use it here."

"Dude, I don't usually see Alva decks around here," the dark-haired guy said. "And what are these, GrindKing trucks? And I haven't even seen these brands of wheels before."

"What a mishmash of parts, and kinda wild, with the different colored wheels," the blond-haired guy said. "You do the work on this board yourself?"

"Yeah," Gavin said. "I've got a closet full of old parts."

"Some impressive work there, keeping it old school," the dark-haired guy said. He handed the board back to Gavin.

Gavin and Lindsey took their pads and helmets. As they walked inside, Gavin thanked Lindsey.

"No problem," she said. "The kids at school don't even think about cash, so I'm not surprised no one told you to bring some. Pay me back when you can."

As he walked into the main area of the indoor part of the
skate park, Gavin was in for another shock. Before him was
a large wooden bowl, about fifty feet across with copings
around the edges. Past that was the halfpipe that he had been
thinking about all day. It was only a twelve-footer, but it was
more ramp than Gavin had ever had a chance to skate on.

Tim walked over to Lindsey and Gavin, and he handed
each of them a number.

"Kyle and Kirk beat us," he said, "so we'll have to wait a
bit."

"Well, let's go watch them skate," Lindsey said.

Gavin liked that idea. He wanted to see what he was getting himself into.

"But we can't get there the easy way," Tim said with a smirk. "Follow me."

Tim planted his skateboard on the rim of the bowl and dropped in. Lindsey followed. Gavin was next. And another game of follow the leader was on.

Tim went up one of the walls and did a nosegrind along the coping, and then dropped back in fakie. Lindsey mimicked him. Then Gavin went up and did the trick.

Next, Tim skated up the side of the bowl and placed one hand on the coping to do a handplant with an mute grab as his feet raised over his head. Lindsey easily mimicked the trick. Gavin hit the handplant, but as he dropped back in, one of his wheels caught on the coping, and he lost his balance. He went skidding across the bottom of the pool on his pads.

As he sat there, he watched Tim skate up to the opposite wall of the pool. He got just enough air to do a nosegrab, and then he landed with both feet on the rim of the pool. On rough pavement, Tim seemed a little shaky. But here, on polished wood, he was smooth.

Lindsey skated up the wall next to him, but she skipped the 180 and just did the nosegrab to pull her board from under her feet as they hit the rim.

"Come on," both of them called to Gavin, who was just getting back on his feet.

The trio got over the halfpipe just in time to see Kyle do a ho-ho, the board resting on his feet while he did a handstand on the coping. Gavin had never seen a trick like that. Then Kyle grabbed his deck, dropped down, and quickly raced up the other end of the halfpipe for a very smooth Madonna to end his run.

"Dang, he's got some slick moves," Gavin said.

Both Lindsey and Tim gave him an odd look.

"*He?*" Lindsey said. "You better get your eyes checked."

Gavin looked up as Kyle stood on top of the halfpipe. He was much thinner than his twin, Kirk. But then Gavin noticed that Kyle's loose T-shirt and baggy khakis hid curves that he hadn't noticed at first. Then Kyle took off *her* helmet, and Gavin saw short-cropped blond hair, and a face punctuated by a nose ring and black mascara. She might not have been wearing a dress, but Kyle was definitely not a he.

"But I thought —" Gavin stumbled over his words as he realized his mistake.

"They're not *identical* twins, ya newb," Lindsey said.

"If you think she's good," Tim said, "watch her brother."

Kirk dropped into the halfpipe. His skating had a totally different vibe. While Kyle was smooth and slick in her moves, Kirk was aggressive. He went for big air from the get-go. His wheels screamed along the ramps as he picked up speed. Higher and higher he went.

He did a casual frontside ollie, and then dropped down the ramp and shot up the other side into a backside air. He kept shooting up the sides of the ramps, getting bigger and bigger air, hardly doing a trick worth mentioning.

"What's so impressive about that?" Gavin asked.

"Just watch," Tim said. "He's getting warmed up."

So he's building up to something, thought Gavin. He watched Kirk closely. He was skating hard, making a loud *CLICK!* every time he landed a trick. Kirk was slamming his wheels down on the wood. Gavin noticed a slight wobble in Kirk's board. To him, it looked as if Kirk's trucks where a little loose for his style of aggressive skating.

When Kirk seemed unable to get any more air, he shot up one side of the ramp and did a smooth frontside ollie. He shot up the other side of the ramp and did a large set-up air. He shot up the other side of the ramp and looked like he was trying for a 540 with an indy grab, but when he came down, a wheel caught hard on the coping, throwing him off balance. He slid down the ramp on his knee and elbow pads.

"He's the only one here who can put down a 540," Tim said.

"Yeah, but all he can do is power moves," Gavin said. "He doesn't have much style."

Kirk stood up and kicked his board across the bottom of the ramp. It skidded over to where Gavin stood. He picked the board up and gave the back wheel that caught on the coping a quick spin and tested the truck. He was right. It was a little wobbly.

As Kirk stomped off the halfpipe in their direction, Gavin held out of the board to him.

"The back truck just needs some tightening," Gavin said.

As Kirk walked by, he knocked the board out of Gavin's hand.

"What do you know? It's a piece of junk," Kirk said. "You might as well keep it. I don't want it."

Kirk stomped off. Gavin turned as he heard a set of feet coming down the stairs to the top of the ramp. It was Kyle.

As she was rushing past him, Gavin said, "Those were some pretty smooth moves. I didn't even know you were a girl at first."

That stopped Kyle dead in her tracks.

"What, girls can't skate?" she snapped. "Just because I'm cute and blond, you think I should be a cheerleader?"

Gavin was totally taken aback. He didn't know what to say, and before he could think of anything, he was lying on his back with Kirk standing over him.

"Leave my sister alone," was all he said. Then he rushed off.

Gavin's temper flared. He jumped to his feet, ready to take off after Kirk and do a little shoving of his own, but Lindsey stepped in front of him. While he had the size on her, she had the attitude.

"Remember Mike? Remember what I said about fighting?" she scolded him. "Check out rule number two."

Lindsey pointed to a big board that hung near the entrance. Rule number two said: No fighting — you will be banned from the skatepark.

"But he started it," Gavin said.

"It doesn't matter," Lindsey shot back. "This is Kirk's turf, not yours. Whatever happens here will be your fault."

The drama completely ruined their skating. Tim went first. His moves were smooth, but he didn't get much air. He did a few grinds and grabs, but not much else. Lindsey was probably the bravest of them. She got a little more air, did a couple handplants, and just missed hitting a backside 540. Gavin was completely off his game. He was shaky the instant he dropped into the halfpipe, so he kept it to simple tricks. But his board nearly slipped out from under his feet on a simple nosegrind. Then, while doing an indy grab, he knocked the board out from under his feet and landed hard on the ramp.

Once Gavin was done with his run, Tim walked off to talk to some friends. Gavin and Lindsey hung around to watch a couple of the other skaters. Tim was right. Most of them were posers. That is, except for Derrek.

Derrek reminded Gavin of a young Tony Hawk. His moves were smooth and natural, as if the board were an extension of his body. He'd skate up one side of the ramp to do a 50-50 axel stall, then dropped back in, shooting up the other side for a nosegrab, letting his skateboard shoot up higher than his head. Derrek's grinds and grabs seemed effortless, and while his tricks weren't as big as Kirk's, he had style. He'd go up one side of the ramp, doing a shuvit into a feeble grind. Then he'd shoot up the other side for a handplant. He didn't even need to grab his board as he dropped back in.

Gavin was impressed.

When they were getting ready to leave, Gavin noticed Kirk's board off to the side. He hadn't seen Kirk since he stomped off, and Gavin was wondering if he really meant it when he said he didn't want the board anymore. Gavin stuffed it in his bag, but he had no intention of keeping it. He just thought he could tweak the board a bit for Kirk. Maybe that would make up for their little run in.

On the bus back to the central bus station, he and Lindsey were pretty quiet. The incident with Kirk seemed to have ruined things. Gavin thought he was cool with Tim, although he was a little standoffish as they said their good-byes. And none of the other skaters at the park even talked to him.

Lindsey nodded at the extra board in Gavin's bag.

"Why'd you take that?" she asked.

"I suppose skate park rule number three is no stealing."

"Actually, it is," she said.

"Any other rules I need to know about?" Gavin asked.

"I think number four is no spitting and number five is no swearing (unless you biff it). That last part was graffitied in."

"Well, so ya know," Gavin said. "I took the board because he didn't want it. Well, actually I took it because all it needs is a little tweaking. These Krux trucks are some of the best, but they're a little too loose for Kirk's style. And he probably doesn't have a hex tool to tighten them. I do."

"What, are you the skateboard fix-it man?"

"Yeah, I am."

MAKING PLANS

Over the next few days, Gavin didn't see much of Tim. He still sat with Lindsey on the bus to and from school at least, but that was about it. He felt as if he was on his own in the new school. He had made a bad impression at the skatepark, and now he was paying for it. Kirk seemed to be a bit of a hero among the skating crew. Even though he was a bit brash, he was an aggressive skater who could hit big tricks that the other kids hadn't even tried.

Then one day, Kyle walked up to him at his locker.

"Hey, you were with Lindsey and Tim on Tuesday, right?" she asked.

"Yeah, I was at the skatepark," Gavin replied.

No one would mistake Kyle for a guy today. A helmet didn't hide her cropped hair. And even though she wore baggy jeans, her wrists were covered in bracelets that clinked and jingled every time she moved her hands.

"Do you have Kirk's board?" she asked. "He didn't really mean you could have it."

"I know," Gavin said. "I picked it up, but I don't plan to keep it. I'm fixing it up for him."

"Why?" she asked. "He treated you like garbage."

"It's what I do," Gavin said. "Fix boards. In my neighborhood, I built all the boards for my crew."

"Seriously?"

"Yeah, it's kinda how I fit in," Gavin said. "They're all into b-ball. One day I was street skating on one of the courts, and they saw me. At first I thought they were going to beat me up for using their court, but they thought what I was doing was cool. So I offered to build them some boards from the spare parts I had lying around."

"What, is your closet like a skateboard garage?"

Gavin blushed.

"I guess that's better than comic books," she said.

"Think I have a few of those in there, too," Gavin admitted. "Mostly Spider-Man."

"Great, a nerd and a skater. What a combo," Kyle said, rolling her eyes. Then with a more serious tone to her voice, she continued. "So here's the deal then. I won't tell Kirk you have his board. He has a few, so he probably won't notice it's missing. Just be sure to bring it by the skate park sometime."

"When will you be there next?"

"Saturday," she said. "Before noon."

After school on the bus, Lindsey looked at him in shock as Gavin told her his plans.

"You can't be serious?"

"Why not?"

"They don't want you there," she said. "Tim was being nice, inviting you along last Tuesday, because you were a fellow skater. But if Kirk doesn't like you, and you snagged his board on top of it, you're nothing to them. None of them, not even Tim, will stand up to Kirk if he has it out for you."

"So does that mean you and your fifteen brothers will come and keep me safe?" Gavin joked.

"That's so not funny."

Gavin was up in his room putting the final touches on Kirk's skateboard. Not only did he tighten the loose truck, but he greased and repacked the bearings on all four wheels. He also added some stiffer bushings. Kirk skated hard, and his board showed the wear.

He actually didn't know why he was going through all this effort for someone who he basically thought was a jerk. *Kirk the Jerk*, Gavin thought. *That has a nice ring to it, but I'm sure I'm not the first to think of it.*

Skateboarding was the one thing that always helped him fit in. The guys he hung out with in his neighborhood were more into b-ball, sure, but it was skating that had gotten him noticed by them. And it was his skills building and repairing boards that had made them friends. Gavin wasn't sure if that would carry over to this new group of kids and his new school, but he was going to give it a shot.

He had moved on to making some minor tweaks to one of his own boards, when he heard the familiar *TWAP! TWAP!* of bouncing basketballs, followed by the rolling of composite wheels on pavement. Gavin grabbed his board and ran for the door.

As he burst out the door, calls of, "G-man!" and, "Gav!" greeted him.

He dropped his board on the landing of the steps that led down to the sidewalk. With a little kick, he gave himself enough momentum to ollie up onto the railing to perform a frontside feeble down its length. He landed the trick perfectly and then skated over to his buds.

"Dang! If only you moved like that on the court."

"Yeah, maybe some Division I school would be scouting you."

Gavin knew he wasn't a perfect fit with this crew, but at least he was accepted for who he was.

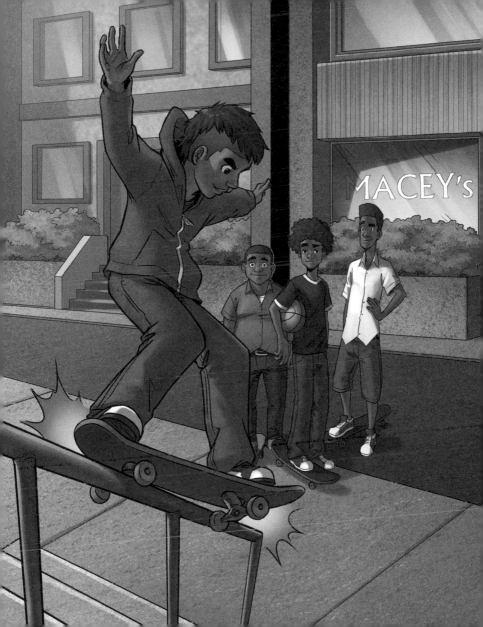

They all pushed their boards forward. As usual, Gavin took the lead. He did a pop shuvit or a kickflip every time he came to a crack in the pavement, and the guys behind would try some version of his tricks to varying degrees of success.

That night, he shot hoops until his legs and arms were numb.

Because Gavin insisted, Lindsey met him at the central
bus station. From there, they took a bus directly to the
Complex.

The Complex had a completely different feel today.
Last time, there had been kids his age, coming straight from
school, filling the place up. Today felt more like a family
day. Little kids wearing shin guards and soccer jerseys were
everywhere. The soccer fields were full of them.

Gavin and Lindsey dodged soccer balls and parents to
make their way over to the entrance of the Complex. No one
was at the front counter of the skate park, but there was sign
that read Reserved for Skate Team Practice.

"What's this?" Gavin asked.

"Kirk, Tim, Derrek, and some of the other kids got their parents to sponsor a skate team," Lindsey said. "They go around the state for competitions. Kirk's actually bragging that he might get a sponsor this year."

"If anyone should get a sponsor, it should be Derrek," Gavin said. "He's got some smooth moves. Or even Kyle."

"Are you crushin' on cheerleader girl?" Lindsey said teasingly.

"You'd better watch it, or I'll talk to Tim for you," Gavin said.

Lindsey went immediately from joking to serious. "Okay, let's just get this over with," she said.

As Gavin and Lindsey entered the arena, they saw about a dozen people around the halfpipe, including some of the kids from school. Kyle, Tim, and the two guys who were working the counter the other day were standing there, watching Kirk skate.

Tim turned and saw them. Both surprise and concern crossed his face. He quickly ran over to meet them. "What are you doing here?" he asked. "The park is closed."

"I brought this for Kirk," Gavin said as he pulled the board from his bag.

"You had his board?"

"Yeah, I fixed it," said Gavin.

As they were talking, neither of them noticed that the arena had gone quiet. But only for a moment.

"What's he doing here?" Kirk's voice boomed, echoing off the walls.

Kirk was done with his run, and he was now stomping toward Gavin.

"Kirk, wait!" Kyle said as she ran after her brother.

Gavin held the board out to Kirk.

"Hey, man, I —" Gavin begin.

"Stole my board!" Kirk yelled. "Yeah, my sister told me."

Kirk snatched the board from Gavin with one hand and pushed him hard with the other. Gavin stumbled backward, nearly falling into the bowl.

Lindsey, all eighty pounds of her, stepped between the two. So did Kyle.

"That's not what I said!" Kyle shouted back at her brother. "I told you he was fixing it for you."

Kyle pushed Kirk, and surprisingly, he backed off. That's when the two guys who worked the counter came over.

"Do we need to remind you kids about rule number two?" the dark-haired guy said while pointing up to the banner where the rules were posted.

"So, what's this all about anyway?" the blond-haired guy broke in. Then, noticing Gavin, he added, "Hey, you're the dude with the Alva deck."

"He's also the *dude* that stole my board," Kirk jumped in. "And rule number three —"

"Kirk, just chill," the dark-haired guy said, and then turning back to Gavin, he asked, "Did you take his board?"

"Well, yeah," Gavin said. "Kirk just left it, so I —"

"But he didn't take it to keep," Lindsey jumped to his rescue.

"He was fixing it up for Kirk," Kyle added.

"Let me see that board," the blond-haired guy said as he took the board from Kirk. "What'd you do, Gavin?"

"While Kirk was skating, I noticed he was a little wobbly," Gavin said. "So I figured the struts were a little loose for his style of skating."

"So, you have a hex tool at home?" the man asked.

"He has a closetful of tools," Kyle jumped in again.

"Yeah, I do," Gavin said. "I also replaced the bushings with some stiffer ones, and I greased and repacked all the bearings in the wheels. A couple were getting a little roughed up."

"Yeah, Kirk is rather hard on his boards," the dark-haired guy said.

"You can't be taking his side on this," Kirk said. "My dad pays for this team."

"It's still *our* skatepark," the dark-haired guy said.

"And he did some nice work on the board," the other man added. "Check it out."

He handed the board to Kirk, who looked dumbly at the trucks.

"I don't see a difference," said Kirk.

"I mean, check it out, as in hit the halfpipe," the man replied.

As everyone was walking over to the halfpipe, Derrek slid next to Gavin.

"Gordy's my dad, and Lee's my uncle," he said.

"Who?" Gavin asked.

Kyle leaned close to him, "Gordy's the blond dude, and Lee's the dark-haired one. They run the skate park."

So that's where Derrek got his old-school slang from. It was a family thing.

Kirk was the first one to the halfpipe. He practically ran up the steps to the top of the ramp. Before anyone could join him, he dropped into the halfpipe.

He was skating hard and doing some frontside airs. He'd go for some big air, and every time he'd drop in, he pushed down on his deck, causing a loud *clunk!* as wheels hit wood.

"What's he doing? Trying to break the thing?" Lindsey asked.

"Nah. He's testing it," Gavin said. "Just wait."

After a couple more runs, Kirk planted a hand on the coping, doing a handstand while grabbing the board with the other hand.

"See, it's on now," Gavin said. "He trusts the board."

Kirk shot up the other end of the ramp, and did a lazy backside 360. Then he went for a couple easy frontside airs. Everyone could feel the energy building.

Kyle leaned in and whispered in Gavin's ear, "He's setting up for something big."

When Kirk came up the other side of the ramp, he shot so high that it seemed like he would never come down. He did an indy grab and then spun around not once, but twice. A 720 indy!

The kids, as well as Gordy and Lee, hooted and hollered.

Kirk was all smiles as he walked off the ramp.

"I guess you know what you're doing," Kirk said as he walked past Gavin. "But that still doesn't give you the right to talk to my sister."

"I'm gonna talk to whomever I want," Kyle shouted as she chased after her brother.

Gavin knew he wasn't going to get an apology out of Kirk. But at least that slight nod of approval would get him back in with the rest of the crew.

Tim stepped up to Gavin as Kirk and Kyle walked off.

"We call them Twin Drama behind their backs," Tim said. "They're always yelling and screaming at one of us or each other."

They shared a laugh.

Gordy stepped up to them as Lee shouted, "Okay everyone, let's get back to practicing. Tim, you're up on the halfpipe!"

"Can I stay and watch?" Lindsey asked.

"As long as you don't distract your man, Tim, there," replied Lee.

Tim and Lindsey blushed at the same time. Gavin could fix boards, but it was going to take some work to fix those two up.

Gordy put one hand on Gavin's shoulder and led him away from the halfpipe.

"I've got a proposal for you, kid."

"For me?"

"Yeah, you, Mr. Fix-it," Gordy said. "You saw all those little soccer rugrats out there. You know what they want to do when they're done kicking each other in the shins? They want to skate."

As they walked around the bowl, Gavin noticed they were walking toward what looked like storage rooms.

"They don't all have boards, so I rent them out for a few bucks a pop."

Gordy opened one of the rooms. Skateboards littered the floor, hung from shelves, and were stacked on crates.

"The little ones are worse than Kirk when it comes to abusing skateboards. At least Kirk can skate. If you help me keep these boards in shape, you can skate here all you want for free. Whenever you want. I'll even set you up wit your own locker. Deal?"

"Can I bring some friends?"

"As long as they follow five simple rules, you can bring whomever you want," Gordy replied.

"Then it's a deal."

THE WHOLE CREW

They were a crew of eight, including Lindsey, on the bus headed over to the Complex. Gavin didn't tell his friends where they were going. He didn't even tell them to bring their boards. He had a few spares set aside for them. All his friends knew was that he had a treat for them.

It took them about an hour to get to the Complex. Gavin's friends were getting a little antsy, seeing that they were deep in the 'burbs. But Lindsey and her smart-alecky wit kept them entertained. Gavin's friends didn't want to seem less tough that this little Hmong girl they'd just met.

Finally, they pulled into the Complex. The soccer fields were full of kids chasing after balls, and their parents cheering for them.

"Is this your school?" one of his friends asked.

"Nah," Gavin replied. "But the school's just a few blocks from here."

"Then where we at?" another friend asked.

"This is the Complex," Gavin said. "And you boys are in for a treat."

They all jumped off the bus, with Lindsey taking the lead, and headed toward the front doors. But before they got there, a couple of the guys were distracted by the outdoor skate park. They ran up to the fence and looked it.

Gavin had to smile. He must have looked just like them, with their eyes wide and slack jaws, the first time he peeked into the skate park.

"Is this where you've been skating?" one friend asked.

"Yeah, it is," Gavin said. "And I'm gonna should you how to drop into a halfpipe."

"No way!"

"Really!" said Gavin.

"This way, boys," Lindsey said, herding the crew inside.

No one was at the counter, but there was a sign saying Reserved for Cole Party.

Gavin jumped behind the counter and started pulling out the gear he had stashed for his friends. Once they were set, they all went inside.

He could tell his friends were tense — just has he had been — seeing the halfpipe on the other side of the arena. They had less experience than he had, but there was no pressure. This was just among friends.

Tim was on top of the halfpipe waiting for them.

"You ready?" Gavin asked.

"Yeah, halfpipe lesson number one," he said, "dropping in."

Gavin's friends from his neighborhood lined up next to the halfpipe while Lindsey went up to join Tim. They shared a quick smile and a blush. Then Tim was all business.

He set his skateboard down with the tail on the rim and the back wheels just over the coping. His right foot held the board in place as he explained what he was doing. Then his left foot came down on the front of the board right above the front truck, and he leaned forward.

Tim went up the opposite side of the ramp, rocked to fakie, and then was back up on the rim where he started. He paused there and invited some of Gavin's crew to try it.

Gavin smiled as he watched his new friends skating with his old ones. Here at the skatepark, they weren't kids from the 'burbs or kids from the city. They were just skaters, doing what skaters do: hanging with friends, carving on the verts, and hitting some tricks.

Gavin Cole's fix-it skills at the Complex have become so valuable that he now earns a salary on top of the free skating privileges. He is thinking about studying mechanical engineering in college with the hopes of building boards from stage one.

L2S Raw

L2S Cole Hawk Face

L2S Mr. Fix-it

SKATE CLINIC:
DROPPING IN

1. At the top of the ramp, take a look and decide which direction you will skate. On a halfpipe, you have just one direction to skate. Other ramps will have more choices.

2. Rest the tail of your board flat on the coping at the edge of the ramp. Hold it in place with your back foot. Once balanced, place your front foot on the deck right over the front trucks. Keep your weight on the back foot.

3. When you are ready, put your weight on the front foot and lean forward. Bend your knees. As the front wheels hit the ramp, balance your weight on both feet. Don't hesitate, or you'll fall backward and slide down the ramp.

4. As you near the bottom of the ramp, you'll have to use your knees to adjust to the change from going down to riding forward.

SKATE CLINIC:
TERMS

50-50 truckstall
a move where the rider rides up a ramp and rests the board on the deck of the ramp with the trucks on the coping

feeble grind
a move where the skater grinds a rail with the back truck, while the front truck hangs over the rail's far side

frontside air
a move where the rider goes up a transition, grabs the board on the toeside between the feet with the trailing hand, lifts off, and turns frontside (toward the skater's back)

grab
a move where the rider holds the skateboard during an aerial trick

ho-ho
a move where the rider does a handstand with both hands on the coping, with the feet fully extended and the board resting on top of the feet

indy grab
a grab where the rider places his or her back hand on the toeside of the board

kickflip
a move where the rider pops the skateboard into the air and flicks it with the front foot to make it flip all the way around in the air before landing on the board again.

nose grab
a grab where the rider grabs the front of the skateboard with the front hand while the feet are in an ollie position

ollie
a move where the rider pops the skateboard into the air with his or her feet

pop shuvit
a move where the skater ollies and spins the board 180 degrees before landing on the board again

shuvit
a move where the skater jumps and spins the board 180 degrees underneath him or her before landing on the board

TONY HAWK
LIVE2SKATE

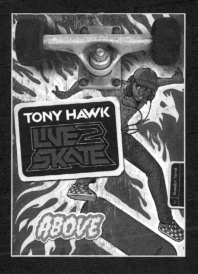

TONY HAWK
LIVE 2 SKATE

ABOVE

by Brandon Terrell

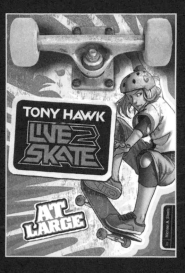

TONY HAWK
LIVE 2 SKATE

AT LARGE

by Michael A. Steele

TONY HAWK
LIVE 2 SKATE

RAW

by Blake A. Hoena

TONY HAWK
LIVE 2 SKATE

STRONG

by Matthew K. Manning

HOW DO YOU **LIVE** ?

written by
BLAKE A. HOENA

Blake A. Hoena grew up in central Wisconsin, where he wrote stories about robots conquering the moon and trolls lumbering around the woods behind his parents' house. He now lives in Minnesota and continues to write about fun things like space aliens and superheroes. Blake has written more than fifty chapter books and graphic novels for children.

pencils and colors by
FERNANDO CANO

Fernando Cano is an all-around artist living in Monterrey, Mexico, currently working as a concept artist for video game company CGbot. Having published with Marvel, DC, Pathfinder, and IDW, he spends his free time playing video games, singing, writing, and above all, drawing!

inks by
OMAR LOZANO

Omar Lozano lives in Monterrey, Mexico, and works in the video game industry as a concept artist. When he was younger, he loved to skate. Now, he enjoys hanging out with friends, watching movies, playing music, and drawing!